The Adventures of
Jake and Moon Granny:

Blackbeard's Revenge

By Jaye Seymour

About DyslexiAssist™

Part of our mission at Knowonder! Publishing is to make literacy more effective. In order to fulfill that mission for children suffering from dyslexia we are proud to announce our new DyslexiAssist™ initiative: to publish each of our books in a special font designed to make reading easier for dyslexics. You can learn more about it on our website at:

www.knowonder.com/dyslexiassist

When reading with this new font, independent research shows that 84% of dyslexics read faster, 77% read with fewer mistakes, and 76% recommend the font to others who suffer from dyslexia.

Reading stories is a highly enjoyable form of entertainment and learning for many people but people with dyslexia have been unable to find joy from books. We hope this new initiative can now bring the same love and joy of reading to your home!

Thank you to Kathy Rygg and the brilliant Knowonder! team, and to my fabulous family.

For Sophie, Georgia & Jessica,
Thom, Joe & Alexander,
Tilda, Bea & my super new
nephew-in-waiting.

Table of Contents

1

A SMELLY SURPRISE

One of the things Jake liked best about trips

into space with Moon Granny was telling everyone

back home about their amazing adventures. He'd

even written a school report on their latest trip,

which had been the most exciting one yet. He and

Granny had flown through a meteor storm, feasted

with the King of Zabalon, and rescued Great Uncle

Raymond from the stinkiest space pirates in the

entire universe.

Jake's classmates listened wide-eyed and open-mouthed as he read his report. His teacher, Miss Flockpockle, seemed less impressed.

"Then," Jake said, "I slugged Blackbeard on the head with the perfume bottle and knocked him out. Granny and I tied him up with wool and waited for the other pirates to arrive so we could swap prisoners. He did look funny lying there like a big green caterpillar. Did I mention the smell? It was unbelievable! Imagine the stinkiest toilet ever, mixed with a bucketful of rotten bananas and fish guts..." Jake caught sight of Miss Flockpockle's face. Her eyebrows were halfway up her forehead, and her mouth was puckered up tight like a monkey sucking lemons.

"I think we'd better leave it there, thank you, Jake," she said in a cross, pinched voice. "A very inventive story I'm sure, with plenty of colorful detail, but the homework was to write a report on a realevent that you enjoyed. Space travel is only for highly-trained adults. And as for this Blackbeard nonsense! What chance would a schoolboy have against a dangerous criminal with a laser pistol? I think you've been playing too many space computer games when you should have been practicing your spelling. Or maybe that pirate history project you did has been giving you strange dreams!"

Jake's cheeks reddened. "But it was real. Every last bit of it. Granny and I rescued Great Uncle Raymond and his pet fire newt, Flamer, and brought them back to Earth for a visit. They've been staying with us all week. It's true," he protested. "Great Uncle Raymond offered to bring Flamer in for 'Show and Tell' but Mum was worried he'd burn the school down."

Miss Flockpockle's eyebrows inched even higher up her face. "Really, Jake, a vivid imagination is all well and good, but I..."

"What about Fluffkyins?" Jake interrupted, desperate to prove he was telling the truth. "She's Blackbeard's prize pet rabbit. He even has a tattoo of her on his arm."

Miss Flockpockle frowned. "Do you mean the rabbit you brought in when I was away on my training course? Why would a bloodthirsty pirate just hand her over to you if she's so precious? That doesn't make any sense."

"It's a bit complicated," Jake said. "Great Uncle Raymond hid Fluffykins in his coat because the pirates had taken Flamer. And then he forgot about her in all the rescue excitement. By the time we got back to Earth it was too late to give her back. I wanted to keep her, but our cat Swish kept chasing her round the garden. Mum said she'd be better off at school with Jefferson and Lincoln."

Jake glanced at the rabbit cage in the corner of the classroom. Jefferson was curled up in a ball, and Lincoln was drinking from the water bottle. "Where is Fluffykins?" he asked. "I can't see her anywhere."

Miss Flockpockle coughed. "She's gone, I'm afraid. There wasn't really room for three rabbits in the cage, and Lincoln kept biting her tail. So I decided it was best if she went to the pet rescue center. I'm sure they'll find her a lovely new home."

One of the girls at the back of the class raised her hand. "But what if the space pirates come looking for her?" she said. "What if Blackbeard wants her back?"

Miss Flockpockle sighed. "For the last time, Jake has not been battling buccaneers in outer space. Even if he had, I imagine any self-respecting pirate crew would have better things to do with their time than chase after a missing rabbit. Now I don't want to hear any more about it."

The girl's hand shot back up. "But Miss Flockpockle, if they don't want their rabbit back, what's he doing here?" She pointed to an ugly-looking brute with spiky grey stubble, standing in the doorway. He wore a patch over one eye and a black bandana with a white skull and crossbones design. The girl pinched her nose. "What's that terrible smell?"

"Poooeeee," one of the boys added. "What a stink!"

Jake took two steps back, clutching onto a nearby desk for support. "Blackbeard!" he gasped in horror. He thought he'd seen the last of that vile villain. "Where did you come from?"

The pirate growled. "Where do you think I came from, you filthy little flea-face? I've been flying round the universe looking for my precious Fluffykins, haven't I?" He pointed to his eye patch with a hairy, black-nailed finger, and growled again.

"Only it's not so easy with just one eye."

"What happened to your other eye?" one of

Jake's classmates asked.

"What happened?" Blackbeard roared. "What

happened? Your friend Jake and his barmy old bat

of a granny — they're what happened. That little

Earthsqueak there sprayed hairspray in my face, and

the doctor says I need to wear a patch for the next

three months 'til it gets better. He didn't tell

you that bit of the story, did he?"

"I ran out of time," Jake explained, trying to keep the tremor out of his voice. What would Blackbeard do when he discovered his rabbit was gone? "And then Miss Flockpockle said..."

"Oh yes," Blackbeard interrupted. "I heard exactly what Miss Flotpottle said. She took my precious Fluffykins to the pet rescue center."

Jake glanced at his teacher. She didn't look at all scared by the appearance of a bloodthirsty pirate in her classroom. She didn't even look surprised.

"That's enough, Mr. Blackbeard, if that really is your name," Miss Flockpockle said in her best telling-off voice. "I'm trying to teach a lesson here, and I won't have it interrupted. Especially not by an unruly, unwashed oaf like you. Do you understand?"

"Be careful," Jake whispered. "He might turn nasty."

"Oh, I'm not afraid of him," Miss Flockpockle said. "It's not even a very good costume. Really, Jake, I don't know what you were thinking. First, you invent a ludicrous tale about kidnapped great uncles and space pirates, and then you drag in an unsavory-looking stranger to disrupt the class all over again. I've never seen a less convincing pirate. I think you should send your friend away and report to the headmaster's office."

"But Miss Flockpockle..." Jake stammered.

"At once," his teacher added.

"Zip it," Blackbeard shouted, waving his fist at Miss Flockpockle. "Handing out insults is my job, you bossy-booted blood-bug. You disbelieving dung beetle. This isn't a costume, I'll have you know, it's the very latest in space pirate fashion. And this," he pulled out a strange, spiked pink cube from his pocket, "is the very latest in space technology — a Meltamax 4000. I stole it from a Disinfectian Army Officer three days ago. And do you know why it's called a Meltamax 4000?" he snarled.

Miss Flockpockle pursed her lips. "No I don't. And what's more I have no wish to know."

"It's called a Meltamax, you tiresome tadpole of a teacher, because it turns your enemies into soft, melty strawberry ice cream. Just one press of this button here — that's all it takes. And it's called a 4000 because...erm..." He peered at the instruction panel on the bottom. "Flobbering flabbersticks, the writing's too small. It's this bloomin' eye patch," he grumbled. "I can't see a thing."

"Perhaps," Miss Flockpockle suggested, "it's called a 4000 because that's the number of days it's been since you last took a bath? Stop stinking up my classroom, you filthy, fancy-dressed fraud, and go, before I have you thrown out."

Blackbeard opened and closed his mouth like a goldfish. "Stop giggling," he warned the girls at the back of the class. "And as for you, Miss Flobpocket, one more word out of your scrawny little mouth and they'll be scooping you up into waffle cones. They'll be squirting strawberry sauce on your head and serving you up for dessert." He waved the Meltamax 4000 around in a menacing manner, and the giggling stopped.

"It's Flockpockle, actually." She wagged her finger in the pirate's face. "You might at least get my name right, you ridiculous, rude little man."

Blackbeard drew himself up to his full height. Jake held his breath.

"Little?" the pirate sneered, towering over Miss

Flockpockle. "LITTLE? Do I look like a little man to

you?" He shook his head in bewilderment. "No

one's ever called me that before...at least, not

since I was little. You've asked for it now, Miss

Flatpack. I hope you like ice cream!" With a mean

pirate laugh that echoed all around the classroom,

Blackbeard pointed the Meltamax 4000 straight at

Jake's teacher and pressed down on the button.

2

CLASSROOM CHAOS

There was a bright pink flash and a short crackling sound like sausages in a frying pan. Jake watched in confusion as Miss Flockpockle put her hand over her heart and smiled. Miss Flockpockle never smiled.

"Well go on then, turn into ice cream," Blackbeard ordered. He gave the Meltamax 4000 an impatient shake. "It should have worked by now."

Miss Flockpockle kept on smiling. "Oh, Mr. Blackbeard," she said in a strange, syrupy voice.

"What *is* that delightful aftershave you're wearing? It smells like sweet spring mornings and blueberry muffins straight from the oven." She took a deep breath. "Such a heavenly scent."

"You what?" Blackbeard grunted, looking from her to the pink cube in his hand. "I don't understand. You should be melting into a sticky pink pool on the floor by now."

Miss Flockpockle giggled. "Oh, Mr. Blackbeard. You *are* funny. And *so* handsome. A picture of pirate perfection!"

Jake and his friends looked at each other. What on earth was going on?

"Are you okay, Miss Flockpockle?" Jake asked.

"Of course I'm okay," she said, "now that this handsome hunk of a hero has arrived to sweep me off my feet." She turned to the bewildered Blackbeard. "You *are* going to sweep me off my feet, aren't you, sweetie pie?"

"Er...ah...um..." Blackbeard stammered. Jake had never seen him so lost for words.

"And I see you've brought your friends along too," Miss Flockpockle added. She pointed to the doorway where three more pirates now stood. "How delightful!"

"Sorry we're late, Blackbeard," the first pirate grunted. "The bossy caretaker bloke said we couldn't just leave the ship in the middle of the schoolyard. He made us park it by the bike sheds

instead."

"Did you find Fluffykins?" asked another.

Blackbeard shook his head. "We're too late, me

hearties. She's already gone. This whining wasp of a

woman took her to the pet rescue center." He

pulled an old, holey sock out of his pocket and

dabbed his eyes with it. "My poor little Fluffykins."

"So what are we waiting for?" the third pirate

asked, whom Jake recognized as Long John Mercury.

He was wearing the same orange spotty trousers as

the week before, and his chin still looked pink and

sore where Flamer had burned his beard off. "Let's

go and get her." He picked his nose and examined

his finger. "I wonder if they've got any nice parrots at the rescue center. I'd like a big green and red one that knows lots of rude words."

"I'm afraid it's a little late for that." Miss Flockpockle smiled again. "They've probably found a new family for Fluffykins already." She threw her arms around Blackbeard's waist. "But don't be sad sweetiekins. You've got *me* now. I'll be your Fluffy-wuffykins."

"Ugh!" Long John Mercury spat, his face wrinkled up in disgust. "Why's that woman talking all lovey-dovey to you, Captain? It's making me feel quite sick."

Blackbeard shook his head. "I don't know. She was being bossy and bothersome so I blasted her with the Meltamax 4000. But she didn't turn into ice cream like she was supposed to. She turned all gushy and gooey instead."

"Revolting," the first pirate said.

"Disgusting," the second agreed.

"Perhaps you didn't read the instructions properly?" Long John Mercury suggested. "Let *me* have a look."

Blackbeard handed him the pink cube, and he held it up to the light.

"Let's see what it says on the label. 'Welcome to your new Meltamax 4000. It offers instant results at any distance up to 25 meters. Simply point and press for an immediate heart-melting reaction — turning hate into love or your money back'.... Curses, Captain. I think you might have got the strawberry ice cream bit wrong."

"Well the Meltamax *3000* certainly turned people into ice cream," Blackbeard argued, "because we used it on the Crown Prince of Jubberjax that time. Remember? Why on earth would they change it?"

"Perhaps the Disinfectian Army had enough of cleaning up after all their fights?" Jake suggested. He'd read about Disinfectia in one of Dad's old space books. Apparently it was one of the tidiest planets in the universe, with an entire branch of the Army dedicated to sweeping and polishing. "This way they can sort out their enemies without the need for fighting *or* a cleaning cloth. It's a brilliant idea."

"It's a *terrible* idea," Blackbeard grumbled. "I wouldn't have bothered stealing it if I'd known. The last thing we want is people*loving* us. We want them quaking in their boots, not baking us cupcakes." He shuddered. "They should be shivering in their shoes, not showering us with 'orrible kisses. A nice bit of hate and fear's what we want...anything but *love*."

"Such a wonderful sense of humor," Miss Flockpockle trilled. "As if anyone could hate and fear a big teddy bear like you!"

"Right, that's it!" Blackbeard yelled. "No one calls *me* a teddy bear and gets away with it. And no one gives my precious rabbit to a pet rescue center either. I'll teach you to mess with Bloodthirsty Blackbeard the Bad, you meddlesome monkeyface. You're coming with us."

"Oh thank you, thank you," Miss Flockpockle said. "It's like a dream come true." She turned back to the class. "Right. I'm off. Get out your math books and work through the sums on page fifty-seven. In silence."

"But Miss Flockpockle," a girl in the front row said. "You can't just leave. We need a teacher to look after us."

"Fine," Miss Flockpockle answered. She pointed to the first pirate. "You there. What's your name?"

"They call me Curly Cutthroat on account of my lovely long curls and my lovely sharp cutlass."

"Okay. Children, this is your new teacher, Mr. Cutthroat. Do exactly as he tells you and no throwing paper airplanes while his back is turned. Do I make myself clear?"

"Yes, Miss Flockpockle," the class chanted.

"But I'm not a teacher," Cutthroat protested. "I'm a rough and tough pirate with bad breath and a nasty rash on my bellybutton."

"You sound perfect." Miss Flockpockle beamed. "Congratulations, you've got the job. Lunchtime is at noon and spelling tests are first thing on Monday mornings."

Cutthroat looked terrified. "But I..."

"I'm afraid you'll have to do as she says," Blackbeard ordered, "'cause we won't all fit on the ship otherwise. We've only got four hammocks on board and I'm certainly not sharing with *her*."

"But I..."

"Don't worry," Blackbeard whispered to

Cutthroat, "I've got a cruel and cunning plan."

Jake inched forward so he could hear. "We'll come

back for you as soon as we've ditched Miss

Frogspawn. I'm going to take her to the

Intergalactic Swap Shop on Switchox and trade her

in for a new rabbit. It's what Fluffkykins would have

wanted. 'Cause pirates don't get mad, they get

even!"

"Brilliant," Long John Mercury said, "that'll

teach her."

"Genius," the other pirate agreed.

"Please don't leave me," Cutthroat begged, but

Blackbeard was already heading for the door with

Miss Flockpockle skipping along behind him.

3

SAVING MUM

Jake and his friends pressed their noses up against the classroom window. This was too good to miss. *Whooosshhh!* The battered black pirate ship zoomed up from the bike sheds like a turbo-charged fly. A ripple of excitement ran through the watching group, and some of the kids clapped and cheered. It wasn't every day the class teacher ran off with a smelly pirate. But not everyone was as pleased to see her go.

"Pluto's pants!" Cutthroat wailed. "I can't believe they left without me. What will I do now?" He stared at the math book in his hands. "None of this makes any sense."

"That's because you're holding it upside down," Jake pointed out. He frowned at the thought of spending the rest of the year with a pirate for a teacher and wondered if he could have done more to stop Miss Flockpockle from leaving. She might be strict and shouty and over-fond of spelling tests, but she always let them out for lunch on time and chose exciting history projects. She certainly didn't deserve to be traded in for a rabbit.

"Bothering burblenewts," the pirate said,

turning the book the right way up. He studied it for

a minute or two, then held it up to his nose and

took a long sniff. "Math sums stink," he declared

at last. "And so do you 'orrible lot. You're too

short and shiny-cheeked. Ugh! Makes me feel sick

just looking at you." He dug an enormous lump of

brown wax out of his right ear and smeared it

across Miss Flockpockle's desk. "I *still* can't

believe they took that blabbering bedbug of a

teacher and left me here," he muttered, pointing a

waxy finger at Jake. "Why didn't you stop them?

You could have sprayed them with hairspray, like

last time."

"I don't *have* any hairspray," Jake protested. "It belongs to Granny."

"And where *is* the batty old bird when we need her?" the pirate said. "Shouldn't she be chasing after them in her spaceship by now?"

"Granny's at home," Jake said. "She and Great Uncle Raymond are leaving this afternoon, so she's giving the ship a bit of a spring clean. But I could go and get her if you want." Granny would know what to do. She always did. Then Jake had a horrible thought. How had Blackbeard found out about Fluffykins? The only people who knew she'd come to school were Jake and his family, which meant the pirate must have forced the information out of them. And Blackbeard wasn't exactly known for his polite manners.

Jake was on his feet again before anyone could stop him. He had to get home and check that Mum and Granny were okay. Great Uncle Raymond had taken Flamer to the zoo for the morning, and Dad was at work, so at least they were safe. But Jake had a horrible image of Mum tied to a kitchen chair. He pictured Blackbeard poking her with wooden spoons or bashing her with the egg whisk to try and make her talk.

"That's it," Cutthroat called after him. "Go and fetch that gruesome gran of yours and tell her I need a lift to Switchox. If Blackbeard's got to stop for petrol on the way we might still catch them."

He turned back to the class. "And as for you lot...erm...I don't know, write a story or something. Make it nice and gory. Plenty of blood and guts. There'll be extra marks for rude words and toilet jokes. On your marks, get set, go!"

Jake didn't have time to hear what his friends thought about that. He slammed the classroom door behind him and raced off through the school.

"Oi, where do you think you're going?" a teacher called out. "No running in the corridors."

"Sorry, sir," Jake panted. "There's been a wooden spoon attack at home! I need to check on my mum." He pushed through the main doors, bounded down the steps two at a time, and tore off

along the road at top speed.

By the time Jake reached the end of his street,

he was exhausted. He forced himself on, hoping

against hope that Mum was okay. But as he

approached his house, his heart sank. The front door

hung off its hinges, and the leaves on Mum's bay

tree were brown and shriveled. Jake guessed the

dreadful pirate pong had been too much for them.

Swish the Cat cowered under the porch, shaking all

over.

"Mum!" Jake called as he tore through the

house. Where was she? What had those beastly

brutes done with her?

The kitchen showed signs of a struggle. There was flour everywhere and a slippery gloop of smashed eggs across the floor. Had they grilled her for information like a human sardine, or baked her into a giant mum muffin? Jake called out again as he headed for the stairs.

"I'm in here!" came a muffled cry. Jake stopped and listened. There it was again. "In the cupboard under the stairs," the voice called.

Jake rushed across the hall and yanked open the door. Poor Mum was trussed up like a turkey, with an old sock taped across her mouth. Jake eased it off one bit at a time.

"Oh thank goodness," Mum spluttered. "That was the cheesiest, grubbiest, stinkiest sock I've EVER come across. I think I must have passed out with the smell. Where are those awful pirates? Are they still here? Don't let them find you..."

"It's fine, Mum." He untied her hands and feet. "They're on their way to a planet called Switchox."

Mum breathed a sigh of relief and crawled out of the cupboard. "Thank goodness for that. I'm not sure my nose will ever recover."

"The only problem is they've got Miss Flockpockle with them," Jake explained. "And they're going to trade her in for a new rabbit." He filled Mum in on the morning's events and her face grew more and more serious.

"It's all my fault," she said. "I should never have told Blackbeard where Fluffykins had gone. But he threatened to take his T-shirt off and release the full whiffy power of his armpits. It was too much for me."

"Don't worry," Jake said. "As long as you're okay. I'm sure Granny will be able to get her back. Where is Granny anyway?"

"Still out in the spaceship, I think. She must have had her stereo on too loud to hear anything."

Jake wondered why the pirates hadn't attacked Granny's ship. Perhaps they were worried she'd wallop them with her handbag again or knit them

into woolly green caterpillars. Or maybe her terrible

taste in music had scared them all away!

He helped Mum into the kitchen, sat her down

at the table, and then rushed off to the garden to

find Granny. Her spaceship sat smack in the middle

of Mum's best flowerbed, pumping loud music out

across the lawn. Or at least it used to be a lawn

— before Flamer burnt it to a frazzled brown crisp.

Their last trip into space had left Granny's ship

scratched and dusty with great streaks of space

gull poo across the roof and windows. But now it

shone and gleamed in the morning sun. Granny had

clearly been busy. Jake knocked on the hatch and

shouted to her above the *boom boom boom* of her

rap music.

"*I'm a go-getting granny from Outer*

Space," Granny sang,

"*Come and hang with me if you can take the*

pace,

I'm swifter than Saturn and I'm mightier than

Mars,

Rocket now, rocket now, zooming to the stars!"

"Granny!" Jake yelled again. "Let me in! It's

an emergency!"

But Granny kept on singing.

"*I'm a pink-haired pensioner — watch me fly,*

Faster than a laser beam, tearing through the

sky,

    Fighting aliens and pirates are my favorite

games,

    'Cause 'Adventure' and 'Excitement' are my

middle names!"

Jake hammered on the hatch and screamed,

"GRANNY! LET ME IN!"

The music stopped. "Jake? Is that you?" The

hatch swung open, and Granny peered out, blinking

in the bright sunlight. "What's all the racket?

You'll scare the neighbors."

"It's Blackbeard," Jake told her. "He's back.

He tied Mum up in the cupboard under the stairs

and took Miss Flockpockle off to Switchox to swap her for a new rabbit."

Granny threw her feather duster up in the air. "Jumping Jupiter! Why didn't you say so? Your poor teacher must be terrified."

"That's just it," Jake said. "She *wanted* to go. Blackbeard zapped her with his Meltamax 4000, and now she's head over heels in love with him. She even likes the way he smells!"

Granny wrinkled her forehead. "Then we've no time to lose. She'll need to take a Meltamin anti-love pill within the next twelve hours or the effects might be permanent."

"Do you mean she'll stay in love with

Blackbeard forever?"

"I'm afraid so. Lucky for us I've got a whole

bottle of them back on the Moon."

"How come?" Jake asked. "Have you been

fighting Disinfectians?"

Granny laughed. "Of course not. But the Moon

Minister sent me with some special Christmas Moon

cheese for the Disinfectian Army General last

winter, and I took some pills with me in case I got

zapped by mistake. I held on to them afterwards,

thinking they might come in handy. We can zip home

and get them on our way to Switchox. Come on,

let's go!"

"*We*?" Jake asked, his eyes shining with excitement. "Do you mean I'm coming with you?"

"Of course you are." Granny grinned. "It's Jake and Moon Granny to the rescue once again!"

4

ZOOMSTER ZOOMING

Mum took a slurp of tea, staring around her ruined kitchen. Now wasn't the best time to ask about dangerous rescue missions, but Jake didn't have much choice.

"You shouldn't be chasing after pirates at your age," Mum said. "They're nothing but trouble. And I don't want you missing any school."

"But Mr. Cutthroat's a pirate too," Jake pointed out. "And he's a *terrible* teacher. He promised us extra marks for gory stories with rude words. If we don't get Miss Flockpockle back soon, the whole class will end up like him. Please, Mum!" he begged. "Otherwise it will be too late to save her."

"Oh all right," Mum said. She took another slurp of tea. "I'm sure it's a bad idea, but after everything's that's happened I'm too tired to argue." She wrinkled up her nose. "I've washed my face four times now, but I can still smell that horrible sock. I'm going to have nightmares about it for weeks."

"Thanks, Mum." Jake grinned, blowing her a kiss as he backed out of the kitchen. "You're the best.

And don't worry — I'll be perfectly safe. Granny

will look after me."

"Exactly," Mum said. "That's what I'm afraid

of."

Jake took a banana out of the fruit bowl and

tucked it into his pocket as he left. A trip to the

Moon probably meant Moon cheese sandwiches for

lunch, and he'd need something to take that sweaty

socks and moldy cabbage taste away afterwards. He

grabbed his space boots from the shoe rack and

raced back to the spaceship. With just eleven hours

left to save Miss Flockpockle, there wasn't time to

pack anything else.

"It's fine," he told Granny as he slid his feet into his space boots. "Mum said I can go."

"Excellent." Granny beamed. "Strap yourself in. First stop, the Moon!"

They counted down together. "Ten, nine, eight, seven, six, five, four, three, two, one, BLAST OFF!"

"Here we go," Jake muttered, bracing himself for the explosion of noise and light.

VVVhhhrrrrrooooommmmm! The spaceship shook and juddered like the wildest roller coaster ever. Jake's stomach lurched, and his head felt as if there were a hundred hammers pounding down on it.

But then everything grew calm and still again, and he knew the worst bit was over.

Granny patted his arm. "I don't know about you, Jakey boy, but I'm ready for some Moonfizz after that."

Jake grinned. "Me too." He stretched over to the shiny yellow button on the control panel and pressed it twice. "Two Moonfizzes coming right up," he said as the round hatch opened up by his feet. A thin metal arm reached out with two bubbling mugs of fruity, fizzy drink on a tray. Jake passed one to Granny and took a long gulp of the other one. "Mmmmm," he murmured, letting the strawberry, raspberry, pineapple, and lemon sherbet flavors fizz and bubble around his mouth. It was so delicious he almost forgot about Miss Flockpockle and their dangerous quest to save her.

"Are we going to use the emergency speed transporter again?" he asked Granny. Jake had discovered it by accident on their last trip into space. One press of the big red button allowed them to cover millions of miles in the blink of an eye.

"I'm afraid not," Granny said. "I found the instruction manual while I was cleaning out the spaceship this morning. It said the speed transporter is strictly for emergencies and runs out after two goes. We've used ours up already, so we'll have to fly the old-fashioned way today. How about a game of *I Spy* to help us pass the time?"

Space I Spy was always fun because there were so many weird and wonderful things to see. Jake spotted a flying kennel filled with barking blue Mutt-Men; a lost-looking school bus from Saturn; a purple Moon cheese lorry setting off on its mid-morning deliveries; and a choir of Mercury mosquitoes singing as they flew by in search of fresh blood. And then, just as he was finishing his second Moonfizz, Jake caught his first glimpse of the Moon.

"Home again." Granny smiled, drinking in the view. "Isn't she beautiful?"

Jake nodded. He hadn't been to Granny's house since he was little and could hardly remember what it looked like.

Granny steered the spaceship in closer until Jake could pick out individual details on the Moon's surface.

"Is that Copernicus?" he asked as they headed for a large crater with stepped walls and impressive peaks in the center.

Granny let out a whistle. "Spot on!" she said. "How did you know that?"

"I've been studying the Moon Atlas you gave me for my birthday," Jake explained as she switched the spaceship into docking mode. "But why are we landing here? I thought you lived further south."

Granny grinned. "Right again, but the parking's terrible at this time of day. It's quicker to leave the ship here and catch the Lunar Zoomster. It's only three stops."

Jake's eyes glinted with excitement. "Is that the underground train with the giant Moon bugs? I've been reading all about them in my fact file."

"That's the one. They're the fastest creatures in the entire universe, so I hope you're ready for a wild ride."

Jake punched the air and let out a whoop of excitement. "You bet!"

They docked the spaceship, and Granny locked

the hatch into place above a steep spiral staircase.

No one walked anywhere on the Moon's surface

without a thick protective outfit and heavy helmet.

During the two weeks of daylight it was hot enough

to boil water. And the two weeks of night made an

Antarctic winter seem warm and toasty.

Underground and air travel were much quicker and

easier.

"This way," Granny called, bounding down the

steps two at a time, leaving Jake following along

behind her. The low-gravity bouncy feeling in his

legs was strange at first, but good fun, once he got

used to it.

Down they went, twisting round and round until Jake felt quite dizzy.

"Are we nearly there?" he called out as a rustling, rumbling sound filled the air.

"Almost," Granny called back. "And there's a Zoomster coming in now. If we slide down the handrail we just might make it."

Jake heaved himself up onto the sleek white handrail and pushed off. *Whhheeeeeeee!* He shot down the last few twists of staircase and landed in a wobbly heap on the platform beside Granny.

"It's the best way to travel," she said with a wink, helping him to his feet. "But don't try it at home. I'm not sure your mum would approve!"

The rumbling sound gave way to a high-pitched whirring noise. There was a blur of light and a rush of wind, and then everything grew still. Jake blinked in disbelief. A long silver capsule now stood waiting at the platform, pulled by a team of ten enormous grey grasshoppers.

"All aboard," they called as a door slid open in the silver capsule. "Next stop Reinhold B."

Jake and Granny leapt on board and hurried to the spare seats in the corner.

"Strap yourself in, quick," Granny said. "When the Zoomster goes, it REALLY goes."

She was right. Jake had only just clicked his belt buckle into place when the warning whistle sounded and they were

off.*Whoooooooosssssshhhhh!* His cheeks were sucked

back toward his ears, and his stomach felt as if

he'd left it behind altogether. At that speed even

talking was tricky.

"Wow! That...really...is...fast," he gasped,

clinging onto the arm rests.

Granny smiled. "You get used to it after a few

years."

Jake looked out of the window, but the blur of

tunnel lights rushing past at such high speed made

his head feel spinny and strange. He glanced around

the carriage at the other passengers instead. Their

faces were buried behind newspapers and books as if

this was a normal, everyday train journey back on Earth.

Granny seemed to be enjoying herself. "It beats the subway, doesn't it?" But then her expression fell. "Blundering Black Holes! I've just realized something. We were in such a hurry I forgot to buy our tickets. If the Mang catches us we're in *big* trouble."

"The who?" Jake asked. There was nothing in his Moon Atlas fact file about a Mang.

Granny lowered her voice. "The Mang on the Moon. He's the Zoomster ticket collector. He has special suction pads on his feet so he doesn't get thrown across the carriage. He also has three heads, ten hands, and a *very* fiery temper. And if there's one thing the Mang hates, it's a passenger without a ticket."

"What will he do to us?" Jake asked.

"I don't know," Granny said, her forehead crinkling with worry. "I've heard some terrible rumors, but I've never forgotten to buy one before. We'll just have to hope he's working on one of the other lines this morning."

Jake crossed his fingers. He didn't like the sound of the Mang one bit.

"Arriving at Reinhold B," the grasshoppers announced through the ceiling speakers. "Next stop Bonpland. Stand clear."

The Zoomster screeched to a halt, and a group

of spotty grey Moon workers raced for the door.

The grasshoppers didn't leave passengers much time

for getting on and off safely.

"Uh-oh," Granny muttered. "Double uh-oh with

Moon cheese on top."

"What is it?" Jake twisted around in his seat

to see what she was looking at.

Three purple heads loomed into view through the

open door, twirling around on their long stringy

necks.

"Tickets, please," said a deep growly voice as

the Mang stepped on board.

5

THE MANG in the MOON

"What do we do now?" Jake asked. "Should we get off and buy a ticket?"

"Too late," Granny said. The doors slid shut and the warning whistle sounded. *Whooooooosssssshhhhhhh!* They were off again. Jake sunk down lower in his seat as the Mang made his way through the train, checking tickets. Maybe Granny would think of a plan in time. Otherwise...

A purple head swung toward Jake's face.

"Tickets, please," it barked. A second head

bobbed in front of Granny while the third floated

behind, grinding its teeth.

"Erm..." Jake said.

"Umm..." Granny added.

"Tickets," repeated the heads.

"I'm afraid we were in such a hurry we forgot to

buy them," Granny explained. Everyone around them

gasped, peering over the tops of their books and

newspapers to watch.

Jake took a deep breath. "We're on an

emergency rescue mission. We have to save my

teacher."

"I don't care if you're saving the whole

universe," chorused the heads. "You still need a

ticket."

"Perhaps we could get one at the next stop?"

Granny suggested.

"Hmmm," the Mang said. "Perhaps. Or perhaps I

could throw you out here and let you crawl to the

next station."

Granny gulped. So did the rest of train. "We

can't crawl through the tunnel," she said. "There

might be Moon rats."

The Mang's heads smiled. They were mean,

sharp-toothed smiles. "There are *definitely* Moon

rats out there," he said. "Hundreds of the things.

And tunnel tics and hairy spiders as big as a Moon cheese."

Jake shivered. He wasn't normally frightened of spiders. But enormous cheese-sized spiders were a different matter altogether.

"They'll nibble our t- t- toes," Granny stammered. Her face was white and her hands shook. Jake had never seen her so scared. Whatever was down those tunnels must be *really* bad. "They'll p-pinch our feet and scurry up our l-legs," she added. "And if they wrap us up in their webbing we'll never get out alive. Just like in that documentary I watched, *When K- Killer Moon Spiders Attack.* I had nightmares for weeks afterwards."

"Yes," nodded all three of the Mang's heads.
"They *are* pretty deadly when they're angry. But
you should have thought of that before you
travelled without a ticket." He laughed. "Don't
worry. It's only sixteen hours to the next station if
you hurry."

"But we don't have that long," Jake gasped.
"Blackbeard has Miss Flockpockle."

The Mang stopped laughing. "Blackbeard, did
you say?"

Jake nodded.

"Not Beastly Blackbeard the Bad, the stinkiest
pirate in the universe?"

Jake nodded again. "Yes, that's him."

"Well why didn't you say so? Anyone who takes on that pongy old pirate is a hero. And I might be able to bend the rules for a hero. Just this once." The Mang sniffed. "It was Blackbeard and his gruesome gang who stole my fourth head. I still miss it terribly, even after all these years. I can't imagine how you humans manage with just one." He blew one of his noses. "How about you pay a three hundred Moon dollar fine and promise to buy a ticket when you get off? Then I'll let you stay on board until your stop."

Granny felt in her pockets for some money. "I'm not sure I have that much," she said, counting out the silvery notes in her hand. "Seventy, eighty,

ninety, no, I'm afraid that's all I've got."

The Mang turned to Jake. "Well what about

you? How much money do you have?"

"None at all, I'm afraid." Jake emptied out his

pockets. "I *do* have a banana, though. It's a bit on

the squashed side, but I'm sure it'll taste okay." He

held it up in the air. "It looks a bit like the Moon,

don't you think? I mean, that's what a New Moon

looks like on Earth."

The Mang's heads licked their lips. "It smells

wonderful. And I *am* rather hungry. I forgot to eat

breakfast again this morning. My fourth head used

to be in charge of remembering mealtimes."

Jake waved the banana under one of the Mang's noses.

"It's a deal," the Mang grinned. "If it's as tasty as you say, then I accept your payment. You can both stay on board until you reach your stop." Four of his hands grabbed the banana and stuffed it into his nearest mouth. He didn't even stop to peel it first. *Chomp, chomp, squelch, chomp.* The Mang finished chewing and wiped his mouth. "Delicious," he said, letting out an enormous belch. "Enjoy the rest of your journey. And good luck with the pirates."

The Mang moved up the train, and Jake breathed a huge sigh of relief.

"That was close," he said.

"A little too close," Granny agreed. "Give me a bloodthirsty pirate any day. But an ugly big Moon rat with horrible green teeth, or a tunnel teeming with Killer Spiders? Ugh, no thank you."

The rest of the journey passed quietly. Granny kept her promise and bought some tickets as soon as they got off. Jake waited for her on a nearby bench — his legs wobbled like Jell-O after the Zoomster ride.

"All done," Granny announced. "Now it's just 584 stairs to climb and we're home."

Jake gulped. "I don't think I can manage that many."

Granny laughed. "I'm only teasing. Lucky for us there's an elevator." She helped Jake over to the shimmering doors at the far end of the platform, and soon they were rocketing back up toward the surface. From there it was a short glass-tunneled walk to Granny's apartment.

"Home, sweet, home," she said, unlocking the front door. "You were only three years old the last time you were here. I don't suppose you remember much about the place?"

Jake shook his head. "No. But I definitely won't forget it again. It's amazing!" He stared around the huge blue-mirrored room at all the awesome alien stuff Granny had collected on her travels. "Whoa, look at those," he said, pointing to the floating 3D family photos. There was Mum, holding her watering can and scowling at the spaceship in the middle of her flowerbed. There was Dad, eating a Moon cheese sandwich and trying to look as if he was enjoying it. Great Uncle Raymond was holding up Mum's burnt hat in a photo of Jake's Christening. And there, above the built in cinema screen, was Jake himself, wearing his

I LOVE MARS T-shirt.

"I'm afraid there's no time for a guided tour today," Granny said, hurrying to the bathroom. "We need to get those pills and go. Grab a quick Moon cheese sandwich while I find them."

Jake pretended not to hear. He was hungry, but

he wasn't *that* hungry. Then he spotted a box of

biscuity, fruity Moonchomps on the kitchen hover-

counter. That was more like it.

"I'll just take some of these Moonchomps for

later," he called out, stuffing them into his pockets.

"Is that okay?" But Granny didn't reply. She was

too busy banging around in the bathroom, opening

and closing cupboards. Jake went to help.

Granny was on her knees, surrounded by piles of

colored jars and silver tubes. "I don't understand

it," she said. "I'm sure I put them in here after my

trip to Disinfectia, just in case I needed them again.

They're in a bobbly pink bottle with...ah! There they

are." She dived into the nearest pile and emerged

with a bumpy heart-shaped bottle. "Let me just

check," she said, holding it up to her face to read

the tiny white print on the back. "Neptune's

Knickers! They're two months past their expiration

date. That's no good." She shook her head. "Even if

I order some more they won't be here until

tomorrow."

Jake looked at his watch. "But we've only got

seven hours left to save Miss Flockpockle. What

are we going to do?"

6

HUNTING for PIRATES

Granny paced up and down the kitchen. "There must be some other way..." she muttered. "I just need to think..."

"What about your neighbors?" Jake suggested. "Perhaps they'll have some spare pills?" Mum always asked the neighbor for sugar when she ran out of it.

"Leaping light-years!" she cried. "Of course. Why didn't I think of that? You're a genius, Jakey boy. I'll run next door and ask Mrs. Raymore. She went to Disinfectia for her summer holiday, so she's bound to have some. Plus it's her day off, so she should be at home." Granny was out the door again before Jake could answer.

He sat down on the silver love seat to wait, thinking about his school friends back on Earth. Would Cutthroat let them out for lunch, or would he keep them all in, just to be mean? Perhaps he would give them horrible pirate jobs to do like scrubbing the floor or cleaning the toilets. Maybe he would teach them rude pirate songs or organize a fight using rulers instead of swords. What would the headmaster say when he found out Miss

Flockpockle had been replaced by a bloodthirsty buccaneer?

"Good news!" Granny called from the doorway. "I've got some more Meltamin pills *and* the key to Mrs. Raymore's spaceship. She says we can borrow it as long as we're careful."

"Why can't we use yours?" Jake asked.

"Because Mrs. Raymore's will get us there ten times as fast," Granny explained. "She's in charge of lighting, if you remember, so she needs a ship that can travel at the speed of light. It means we can zoom across to the Venus Zip Tube and be at Switchox in just under two hours. We might even get there before Blackbeard!"

Jake realized it also meant they didn't have to travel back on the Zoomster, which was a relief. High-speed lunar travel hadn't been quite as much fun as he thought. And he certainly wouldn't miss all the steps back up to Granny's spaceship.

"Off we go then," Granny said, leading the way to an impressive yellow ship at the end of the entrance tunnel. It was big and round, with yellow-tinted windows and four yellow coiled legs like enormous springs. Everything was yellow inside too, from the strange egg-like seat pods to the enormous floating screen above the control panel.

"I think I know what Mrs. Raymore's favorite color is." Jake laughed. "Is *she* yellow too?"

"Of course not." Granny winked. "But her cat is!"

They climbed into the seat pods, which were comfier than they looked, and strapped themselves in. Granny stared at the buttons on the control panel and scratched her head.

"Have you ever driven a ship like this before?" Jake asked.

"No. But I'm sure it's easy enough. Once I find the 'ON' switch."

"How about this switch here?" Jake suggested, pointing to a small lever marked VOICE CONTROL ACTIVATION. Granny nodded, and he flicked it downwards. Two butter-colored eyes appeared on the screen in front of them, blinking slowly.

"Voice control activated," a loud metallic voice said. The eyes grew larger. "Wait a minute. You're not Mrs. Raymore."

"No," Granny agreed. "But she said I could borrow her ship to take us to Switchox. It's an emergency."

"Really? What's the password?" the voice asked.

Granny shrugged. "Oh dear. She didn't mention anything about a password."

"Is it 'yellow' by any chance?" Jake asked the eyes.

"Correct!" The eyes were joined by a neat round nose and a big smiling mouth. "Welcome aboard. My name is AMARILLO, but Mrs. Raymore calls me Rillo for short."

"What does that stand for?" Jake asked. "No, wait, let me guess. I love acronyms. Is it 'Artificial Mother with Additional'...?"

"No," Rillo cut in, "my name has nothing to do with artificial mothers."

"How about 'Animated Monkey with Advanced Recall'...and then something to do with Iguanas? Or Insects? Or Ice cream?"

Rillo frowned. "Who are you calling a monkey?"

"Sorry," Jake said. "I didn't mean to offend you. Okay, I give up. What does AMARILLO stand for?"

"It's the Spanish word for 'yellow', sir," Rillo said. "Don't they teach you Spanish in school?"

"I'm afraid Miss Flockpockle won't be able to teach Jake anything unless we hurry up and rescue her," Granny said. "Tell me. How do we fly this thing?"

Rillo smiled. "It couldn't be easier. The auto pilot button is the big square one to your left. Just tell me where you want to go."

Granny pressed it, and the entire control panel began to glow. "Switchox, please. The fast route."

"Excellent," Rillo said. "Next stop Switchox, via the Venus Zip Tube. Enjoy the ride. Take off in five, four, three, two, one..."

Jake shut his eyes and braced himself for the explosion of noise and light, but it never came. Instead he and Granny found themselves gliding through space. The autopilot even made Granny a cup of tea.

"And would you care for a Moonfizz, sir?" Rillo asked Jake.

He nodded, and a long yellow tube dropped down from the ceiling until it was level with his mouth. He gave it a cautious suck. "Wow! It really is Moonfizz. This spaceship is amazing! You should get one like this, Granny."

She smiled. "It's a little too smooth for my liking. I prefer a few bumps and bruises when I'm flying. It makes it more exciting."

Jake wasn't convinced. He loved everything about Mrs. Raymore's yellow ship, from the built-in jukebox (with six million songs to choose from) to the onboard sweets machine. One press of the button and the machine pumped out tiny yellow bubbles for him to catch in his mouth. They fizzled on his tongue like popping candy and tasted of cherry-lemon cola. Delicious!

"We are now entering the Venus Zip Tube," Rillo announced. "Estimated time to arrival is one hour forty minutes."

Jake unwrapped a Moonchomp and handed one to Granny. "*This* is the way to travel." He grinned. "The only thing missing is the cartoon channel!"

"Coming right up, sir," Rillo replied. "Please select your choice from the following menu." A list of cartoons scrolled down the screen in front of him.

"Whoa! I was only joking. This is incredible!" Jake chose *Mutant Space Snails* and settled back in his seat with a sigh of happiness. But halfway through the second episode the picture suddenly froze, leaving Slavina the Evil Space Slug hanging in mid-air. The sound cut out mid-slug scream.

"Uh-oh," Rillo said, reappearing on the screen in front of Slavina. "I don't like the look of that."

"What's wrong?" Granny asked. "Is there a problem with the power?"

There was a soft sucking sound, and Slavina the Evil Space Slug disappeared. "The power's fine," Rillo answered. "For now. But I'm afraid we've got a visitor."

Jake guessed it wasn't a *good* visitor. "Is it a pirate?" Perhaps Blackbeard had run out of fuel on the way to Switchox and was hoping to steal some of theirs. It would be the perfect chance to rescue Miss Flockpockle.

Rillo frowned. "Much worse. It's a splimpet. And right now it's only thirty centimeters away from the external power drive. If it gets in there it'll be 'goodbye spaceship'."

"Let's not panic yet," Granny said, although the color had drained out of her cheeks. "We just need to think of a plan."

"I don't even know what a splimpet *is*," Jake pointed out.

"It's a space limpet," she explained. "A bit like a leech. Once they have a hold of you or your spaceship they *never* want to let go."

Jake tried to think of different ways to remove a leech without touching it. "What if we put on some really loud music?" suggested Jake. "The vibrations might shake it off."

"Now *that's* an idea," Granny said. "Good thinking, Jakey boy. What's the worst tune on the jukebox? Something a splimpet would really hate?"

Jake scanned through the list of songs. "How about *Worm Hole Horror* by The Martian Maniacs?"

"Too slow," Granny said. "What else is there?"

"*Meteor Madness* by the Venus Vikings? *Rocking all Over the Universe* by the Caterwauling Comets?"

"Perfect," Granny said. "Let's have some Caterwauling Comets at top volume. If that doesn't shake the creature off, nothing will."

Jake selected the song and put his hands over his ears as the first deafening notes pounded through the ship's speakers. The guitars at the start were bad enough, but the singing was even worse. It sounded like an army of cats having their tails pulled. Or a thousand dogs whining and barking for their owners at the same time. The noise thumped around Jake's skull until he thought his ear drums might explode. But Granny seemed to be enjoying it. She was even singing along!

After three of the longest minutes of Jake's

life, the song finally ended.

"Has that done the trick?" Granny asked Rillo.

At least Jake thought that's what she said from

reading her lips. He couldn't actually hear anything.

It was like being inside a tunnel.

"No," mouthed Rillo. "It's still there."

Granny turned to Jake. "Are you okay?" she

asked.

Jake shook his head. "I THINK THE MUSIC

HAS DEAFENED ME!" he shouted. "I CAN'T

EVEN HEAR *MYSELF.*"

Granny nodded. *She* seemed absolutely fine.

Maybe that was because she always played her

music at top volume. Jake guessed her ears were used to it by now. He saw her mouthing something to Rillo and then a keyboard opened up in the control panel. A message appeared on the screen as she began to type: **Don't worry. It won't last long.**

"WHAT ARE WE GOING TO DO NOW?" Jake yelled.

More text appeared on the screen, but it wasn't Granny typing this time. Jake assumed it was a message from Rillo: **One of you will have to go out there and peel it off. It's the only way to save the ship. The splimpet's only twenty centimeters away from the external drive now.**

"OUT *THERE*?" Jake pointed through the yellow-colored windows. Outside in the Zip Tube everything was spinning and twisting at an alarming rate. "ISN'T THAT REALLY DANGEROUS?"

Granny nodded and typed: **All ships are fitted with an emergency suction suit for carrying out mid-flight repairs. I'm not sure if it will hold my weight traveling at this speed though.**

More writing appeared on the screen. It was another message from Rillo: **You should do it, sir. You're lighter.**

No, wrote Granny. **It's too risky. We'll have to think of something else.**

Rillo frowned. **Splimpet seventeen centimeters** away.

Jake took a deep breath. It wasn't just a question of saving Miss Flockpockle now. If he didn't act quickly, he and Granny would be in grave danger too.

"THERE'S NO TIME FOR ANYTHING ELSE," he yelled. "I'LL DO IT."

7

A WALK on the WILD SIDE

"Your mum would probably faint if she knew what you were doing," Granny said as she helped Jake into the suction suit. "I'm supposed to be looking after you."

"I'm the best chance we've got," Jake pointed out. His hearing was coming back now, although Granny still sounded like she was whispering. "If that splimpet reaches the external drive and short circuits the ship, we'll all be in trouble."

"You're the bravest boy ever," Granny told him, zipping up his space suit and closing the seals on his helmet. Her voice filtered through the helmet's speaker system. "I'm very proud of you."

Jake nodded, although he felt about as brave as a jellyfish. "I must take after my grandmother," he told her, trying to calm his shaking hands. Would the suit hold his weight? He was a whole Moonchomp heavier than he was before.

He read through the instructions on the screen:

1) Only move one hand or foot at a time using a sliding motion.

2) Keep your body as close to the ship as possible.

3) Detach the splimpet using the special space spatula.

4) Watch out for flying zip nippers.

5) Good luck!

Jake bit down on his bottom lip as the first hatch clicked shut behind him. He knew Granny was on the other side of the door, but she seemed a world away. And it felt like an entire lifetime since he last saw his school friends. A morning of math sums with a curly-haired pirate didn't seem so bad all of a sudden. He waited for the green safety light to come on and opened the outer hatch.

Whhhrrrrrrrrr! The inside of the Zip Tube was a twisting, spinning whirl of color and noise. Jake could feel the full force of its light-speed winds

even through the triple layers of his suction suit.

But he did his best to stay calm, moving out one

hand, then the other, followed by each foot in turn.

He felt like a human spider, clinging to the side of

a giant yellow bathtub.

It wasn't until the second hatch closed behind

him that Jake realized he didn't know what a flying

zip nipper was. But he *could* just make out the

splimpet clinging to the side of the ship. He inched

closer.

"You're doing brilliantly," Granny whispered

through the helmet speaker. "I'm watching you on

the screen. You're almost there. Can you see it

yet?"

"It looks like a black jelly blob from here," Jake

answered, his voice echoing in his helmet.

"That's what it looks like close up as well,"

Granny answered. "Keep going. It's ten centimeters

away from the external drive now."

Jake picked up the pace a little, trying not to

look down. Below him lay a twirling, swirling

nothingness. He fixed his eyes on the splimpet

instead. Not much farther.

"Okay," Granny said. "You should be able to

reach it with the space spatula from there. This is

the tricky bit so take it steady. You need to flick it

away from the spaceship, making sure it's clear of the external drive."

"Got it," Jake said. He sometimes helped Mum toss the pancakes at breakfast, so he knew what to do. Only it was much harder with the spatula strapped to his arm and his hand glued to the ship by super strong suction. He couldn't afford to pull his hand away or he might fly off into the Zip Tube.

His first attempt missed completely. He tried to ignore his pounding heart. There was still time for another shot. Maybe it would help if he got a bit closer.

"It's only five centimeters away from the drive now," Granny said. "Keep trying."

Jake took a deep breath. This wasn't a matter of life and death, he told himself. It was just another morning flipping pancakes. All he had to do was slide his spatula under the black jelly blob and *flick!* It worked! The splimpet went flying back over Jake's shoulder and landed *splat* on his back, knocking him into the side of the spaceship. Everything turned dark.

"Are you okay?" Granny asked. "Can you still hear me?"

Jake groaned. His head was spinning, and he couldn't get his eyes to focus. "What happened?"

"You've been splimped," Granny said. "You bashed your helmet on the side of the ship and it's given you a nasty knock. You're going to be all right, Jake," she promised. "But I need you to stay awake and get back inside."

Jake tried to nod but it hurt too much. "What about the splimpet? Is it still on my back?

"We'll worry about that later," Granny said. "Just come back now. That's it, right hand first. Now your left." She guided him toward the hatch. "Watch out for that zip nipper!" Something green and blurry shot past with a loud buzzing noise. "Phew, that was close," Granny said. "You don't want to get on the wrong side of one of those. Its sting is as big as a man's arm!"

Relief flooded through Jake's body when he reached the hatch. Safe at last! Granny released the outer door, and he slid each hand and foot inside. There were four loud *pop*s as the suction pads came free.

"Just a quick spray next," Granny said as a row of tiny nozzles sprung out of the wall. Blue jets of steam squirted at Jake. "We need to make sure you haven't picked up any nasty space bugs out there," she explained.

Finally the steam cleared and the inner hatch swung open. Jake staggered inside.

"Well done!" Granny cheered. "You were amazing."

"Very good, sir," Rillo agreed. "Please remove the suction suit and return to your seat pod. I have programmed it to run a full medical check."

Granny peeled the splimpet off Jake's back with the spatula and squished it into an enormous collecting jar. "It'll be all right in there for now," she said. "Until we can think what to do with it." Then she helped Jake out of his suit and helmet and guided him back to his seat. "I think another Moonfizz might be in order," she said, and the yellow tube dropped down from the ceiling again.

It was amazing how much better Jake felt after a drink and a sit-down. His head cleared, and his vision returned to normal.

The seat pod whirred and clicked around him as it performed its tests, but he didn't mind. He was just glad to be back inside, safe and sound.

Rillo gave a big smile. "Testing complete. You'll be fine, sir, once you've had a good rest. We'll wake you up when we get to Switchox."

"What?" Jake asked as a delicious scent wafted through the top of his pod. It was like vanilla ice cream and lemon sprinkles mixed with Christmas pudding and the smell of cut grass. "But I'm not even tired..." Or at least that's what he meant to say. He got as far as 'not even' and fell asleep.

8

BLACKBEARD'S SHIP

Jake felt Granny shaking him awake.

"We're there," she said.

"What...where...when?" Jake mumbled, feeling

groggy. He stared around Mrs. Raymore's ship in

confusion.

"I must have fallen asleep," he said. "But I

wasn't even tired."

"That was the Saturn Sleeping Scent," Rillo

explained. "A few sniffs of that and you were out

like a light. It's powerful stuff."

Jake rubbed his eyes. "It must be. Still, I feel much better after a rest. I'm ready to save Miss Flockpockle now. Or at least I will be once I've had another Moonchomp."

Granny smiled. "Make it quick then. I've just checked the ship-locator and it looks like Blackbeard might already be here. It's no good bringing the Meltamin pill for your teacher if she's already been traded in for a rabbit."

Jake gobbled down his bar and said goodbye to Rillo.

"Good luck," the computer answered. "You're going to need it!"

Switchox was a very strange-looking planet. Everything had been switched from its proper place; Teacups rested on top of drooping flower stems; grass grew down in thick green tufts above their heads; fish swam through the air, barking to each other; and Jake even spotted a man with giant spoons for legs.

"This is the weirdest place," he told Granny. "Why's everything so jumbled up?"

She shrugged. "I don't know. That's the way it's always been. I guess Earth would seem just as crazy and mixed up to a Switchoxian."

Jake stared around in disbelief as he followed Granny across the enormous landing field.

"Blackbeard's ship should be just over here,"

she called to him, pointing to a large cluster of

matching black spacecraft. Every single one was

painted with a white skull and crossbones.

Jake gasped. "I didn't realize there were so

many pirates in space. What are they all doing

here?"

"They come to Switchox to swap their stolen

treasure," explained Granny. "They even trade it for

food and drink sometimes, if their supplies are

getting low."

"I'm guessing they never swap it for deodorant."

Granny laughed. "Blackbeard certainly doesn't.

But that makes it easier for us to track him down.

If he *is* here already we just need to follow our

noses."

Jake sniffed the air as they approached the first

pirate ship. It smelled like damp raincoats and

three-day old egg sandwiches.

He shook his head and walked on. "That one's

much too nice."

There was a faint whiff of sweaty sneakers and

burnt onions around the second one, and the third

smelled of seaweed and blocked sinks.

"Not nearly stinky enough," Granny said,

holding her nose.

Jake couldn't decide what the fourth ship

smelled like, but there was no mistaking the fifth

one. The stench hit him from a distance half a football field away. It was like walking into a solid wall of rotten bananas and cheesy feet with a few moldy fish guts thrown in for good measure.

That *had* to be Blackbeard's spaceship.

"Found it!" he and Granny both whispered at once. They crept closer, staying low so no one on the ship would be able to see them.

"Do you have a plan?" Jake asked, his heart thumping in his chest. He hoped it was a good one.

"Our first job is to find out if Miss Flockpockle is still on board," Granny said. "And then we'll have to decide how to sneak her off again without anyone noticing."

She made it sound easy, but Jake wasn't so sure. Until she swallowed the Meltamin pill, Miss Flockpockle wouldn't even *want* to be rescued. If they tried to steal her away from under Blackbeard's nose, she'd probably raise the alarm herself. And then there'd be laser pistols and cutlasses to deal with on top of the terrible pirate stench.

"Don't worry, I've come prepared this time," Granny said, patting her trusty red handbag. There was still a slight mark on one side where Flamer had burnt a hole through it, but Mum had done a pretty good job of patching it up. Jake wondered what new weapons were stowed away inside.

Hopefully something a bit better than hairspray and extra sticky toffees.

Granny opened it up and pulled out two of Mum's clothespins. "Catch!" She tossed one to Jake and clipped the other over her nose. "Ah yes," she squeaked. "That's much better. I can't smell a thing now."

It wasn't quite the water blaster or catapult Jake had been hoping for, but at least now he wouldn't have to fight *and* hold his nose at the same time. He slipped on the pin and peered into one of the blacked-out windows. It was impossible to see anything through the dark glass.

Granny shook her head. "I'll try the door. Blackbeard might just be stupid enough to leave it unlocked." She crept up to the hatch and tugged at the release handle. Jake held his breath. To his amazement, the hatch swung open with a soft creak and the landing steps unfolded toward the ground.

"That could do with a bit of oil," Granny said, flattening herself against the wall like police officers did on TV, in case anyone started shooting. But there were no red laser streaks, no pirate roars of rage, no thundering footsteps. Nothing moved.

"Maybe they've already gone," she whispered.

"We'd better just check." She gestured for Jake to follow her and crept up the steps.

It was dark on board, and it took a while for

Jake's eyes to adjust. A thin dribble of daylight

filtered through the black windows, revealing a

disgusting mess of half-eaten take-out cartons and

dirty socks. A pair of filthy grey underpants dangled

from the steering lever, and someone had written

'OI! STOP SPITTING IN MY MILK' in ketchup

across the fridge door. At least Jake *hoped* it was

ketchup. Someone else had scrawled 'ONLY IF YOU

STOP FARTING IN THE BUTTER' underneath, in

what looked suspiciously like earwax.

"It doesn't seem like anyone's home," Jake said.

He couldn't help feeling relieved. "Maybe we'll be

lucky and find Miss Flockpockle locked in the

bathroom. Then we can grab her and go before

Blackbeard gets back."

"It's worth a try." Granny stepped over a pile

of apple cores and toenail clippings. "You try that

door and I'll check this one."

Jake pushed open the rusty-looking door to his

left — or at least he tried to. There was something,

or someone, blocking the doorway.*Uh-oh*, he

thought, jumping back. *I hope it's not a sleeping*

pirate because he won't be sleeping anymore! He

waited for a few seconds, but nothing

happened. *Phew!* He tried again, pushing a little

harder this time.

There was an odd rustling sound as he forced the door open far enough to stick his head through. Jake looked down to see a huge pile of crumpled notes blocking the way. Was one of the pirates writing a book, perhaps? Or was it a collection of old shopping lists? He picked one up and unfolded it. The handwriting was in bright red ink and looked familiar.

To My Gorgeously Handsome Blackbeard,

It's no good pretending you don't love me too. I can see it in those big dark eyes of yours. Even the one with the patch over it. I can hear it in your voice every time you say, "Get off me, you weasely witch," or, "Leave me alone, you blithering bat dropping." You always think of such lovely poetic names for me, you clever man. That's just one of the three thousand and eighty-four things I love about you.

Today has been the happiest day of my entire life — and the nicest smelling too. You should bottle your special pirate fragrance and sell it.

Eternally yours,

Fiona Flockpockle

xxxxxxxxxxxxxxxxxxxxxxxxxxxxxxxxxxxxxxxxxxx

Poor Miss Flockpockle. The sooner they got that pill to her the better. Jake stuffed the letter into his pocket, kicked the other papers out of the way, and scanned the room. Four filthy hammocks hung from the ceiling, with a bent basketball hoop

clinging to the wall behind them. There were more

of Miss Flockpockle's love letters lying in a broken

suitcase, but no sign of the teacher herself. Jake

was just about to go and report to Granny when

something else caught his eye—something round and

purple peeking out from the cluster of cobwebs

below the hoop. Was it a Moon cheese?

Jake brushed away some of the dust and

gasped. Two yellow eyes stared back at him.

"I suppose *you've* come to shoot some hoops

with me as well," a voice said. Where had Jake

heard it before? He thought for a moment, playing

back the day's adventures in his mind. Of course —
that was it!

"No, I've come to rescue you," Jake said. "The
Mang told us Blackbeard had stolen one of his
heads. I'm guessing you're Number Four."

The head blew dust out of its mouth and
coughed. "Yes, I used to be his favorite head of all.
But I thought he must have forgotten about me. It's
been so long. All these years being bounced around
like a basketball." It sniffed. "No wonder I've
always got a headache."

"Did you see what happened to Miss
Flockpockle?" Jake asked. "Is she still here?"

"No," Number Four answered. "They left about twenty minutes ago. Blackbeard wanted to stop for some lunch before they went to the Switchox Swap Shop. I think he said something about the Buccaneer's Burger Bar."

Jake glanced at his watch. "We'd better hurry then. I'll drop you off at Mrs. Raymore's ship on the way — you'll be safe there."

"Thank you," Number Four said, his mouth cracking open in a grateful grin. Jake guessed it was the first smile in a long, long time.

9

FAST FOOD FIGHTING

Jake and Granny dropped off the Mang's head and hurried on their way.

"How far is it to the Burger Bar?" Jake asked, taking the clothespin off his nose. "Have you been there before?"

Granny shuddered. "No, it's a 'pirates only' place. Most people keep as far away as possible. But we must be nearly there now. Listen."

The roar of noise up ahead was growing louder all the time. Soon they heard snippets of conversation amongst the general hubbub.

"Oi!" someone shouted. "Watch what you're doing with that pickle, you nit-nibbling nincompoop! You almost took my eye out."

"Well stop putting onion rings in my ear then."

"It wasn't an onion ring, it was a lump of bellybutton fluff."

"Oh, Mr. Blackbeard," came Miss Flockpockle's voice. Jake would recognize it anywhere. "I'd *love* some of your beautiful bellybutton fluff. Do you have any more? I can sleep with it under my pillow and dream sweet dreams about our wedding day."

"Be quiet, you sniveling snot-bucket, and drink up your water. You're putting me off my lunch. The sooner we get rid of you the better. If only this bloomin' Meltamax 4000 had turned you into ice cream, we could have saved ourselves a lot of trouble. And we wouldn't have to order any dessert either."

"Watch what you're doing with that machine, Captain," Long John Mercury said. "Don't keep pointing it around like that. You know what happened last time."

Jake and Granny stared up at the Buccaneer's Burger Bar. The walls were painted black with a dirty white burger and crossbones sign chalked across the cracked roof. The high, broken windows were boarded up, and green crabs scuttled in and out of the cracks like lizards. Apart from the fish perched on the cotton candy chimney pot, the place looked surprisingly normal for Switchox.

"Are we going in?" Jake asked.

"Not if we can help it," Granny said with a shudder. "Pirates are hot-tempered creatures at the best of times. They're even worse when they're eating. If we barge on in without a proper plan we might not live to tell the tale."

"Look, there's a gap in the wood over that window," Jake pointed out. "If you lift me up on your shoulders I might be able to see in."

"Good idea, Jakey boy," Granny agreed, flexing her muscles. "I'm feeling pretty fit today. It must be your mum's homemade oatmeal. I had four bowls for breakfast."

They tiptoed along the wall until they reached the window. The wood rattled against the pane as a burst of pirate laughter rang out.

"Whatever you do, don't let them see you," Granny told Jake as he hoisted himself up with the help of a nearby teacup flower and balanced his feet on Granny's shoulders. "Jumping Jupiter," she added, clutching at his ankles to steady herself.

"I'd forgotten how heavy you're getting! What can you see?"

Jake pressed his nose to the window boarding and peered in through the gap. It seemed to be the day for peeking in at pirates. But the Burger Bar was better than Blackbeard's ship — this time Jake could actually see what was on the other side.

"We're in luck," he whispered. "I've got a great view of them! Blackbeard's busy picking his teeth and throwing fries at the barmaid. Long John Mercury's blowing milkshake bubbles through a straw, and the other one seems to be asleep with his head in a big bowl of coleslaw."

"What about Miss Flockpockle? Is she there?"

"Yes, I can see her too! She's sitting quietly in the corner, drinking a glass of water."

"Excellent." Granny grunted. Jake guessed he was getting rather heavy. "Now we just need to get that Meltamin pill to her somehow."

"I should be able to throw it in her water from here," Jake said. "But it'll be tricky to do it without anyone noticing."

"You leave that bit to me," Granny told him. "Hold still while I get a pill out of my pocket." Jake could feel her fumbling around inside her spacesuit. There were a few more grunts and mutterings and then at last she whispered, "Got it." She handed him a squidgy blue pill the size of a bean. "Ready? On the count of three. One...two...three!"

Jake launched the pill through the gap in the window, aiming for Miss Flockpockle's drink. At the same time, Granny cupped her hands over her mouth and yelled, "Look out, Blackbeard just spat in your potato salad!" in a deep rough pirate voice.

"I did not!" Blackbeard protested, thumping Long John Mercury on the nose. No one even noticed the pill landing *plop* in Miss Flockpockle's water. Jake watched it fizz and dissolve as Long John Mercury shoved a thick-cut fry up Blackbeard's left nostril.

"Right!" Blackbeard roared. "You asked for it, you scurvy-faced skunk. Take this!" He launched an entire bottle of ketchup across the table. Long John Mercury ducked, and the ketchup flew right over his head into the next booth.

"Which one of you ratty rapscallions did that?" bellowed an enormous pirate, staggering to his feet. His thick red hair and spotty face were dripping with ketchup. "I'll get the lot of you!" he yelled and shot back at Blackbeard's crew with half-eaten corn cobs. Unfortunately his aim wasn't too good, and soon there were angry pirates all over the restaurant, clutching at their heads and roaring.

"Do be careful, Mr. Blackbeard," Miss Flockpockle said. "I couldn't bear it if anything happened to you." She took a long drink of water.

That's it, thought Jake. *Finish it up.*

Food went flying in all directions. And so did the insults.

"Take that, you lily-livered lumpfish!"

"Why, you brainless baboon bottom! I'll teach you to throw barbecue sauce down *my* neck."

"You wimp-faced warble fly."

"You lousy locust."

"You dozy, dribbling donkey brain."

Clatter! Splat! Fries and pickles rained down on a hundred unwashed heads.

"Watch out for that burger bun, Mr. Blackbeard!" Miss Flockpockle gave a nervous cry and polished off the rest of her drink. Jake gave Granny the thumbs up sign.

"Thank goodness," Granny puffed. "I don't think I can hold you much longer."

Jake slithered down, and Granny stretched out her back with a long sigh. "I'll have to try out the massage setting on my seat pod when we get back to the ship." She pointed up to the Burger Bar window. "How's it looking in there?"

"Terrible!" Jake grinned. "There's food *everywhere*. Blackbeard's wearing half a bucket of chicken wings on his head, and Long John

Mercury's got a new coleslaw beard!"

Granny giggled. "Perfect! Now we just need to

wait for the pill to take effect so we can get your

teacher out of there. It should be any minute now."

She was right. Just then a loud cry rang out

across the squabbling pirates.

"What do you think you're doing?" Miss

Flockpockle shouted in her best telling-off voice.

"Sit down at once, all of you, or there'll be

trouble."

The Burger Bar fell silent, as if the pirates had

forgotten they were rough, tough villains who

weren't afraid of anything.

"Er...yes, Miss," came a few gruff replies.

"Sorry, Miss."

"Now then," the teacher's voice rang out across the diner. "Would someone like to tell me what's been going on?"

"Blackbeard started it."

"No I didn't."

"Did so."

"Didn't."

Miss Flockpockle cleared her throat. "That's quite enough of that, thank you very much. I don't care *who* started it. I just want to know where I am and how I got here. And what on earth is that*dreadful* smell?"

"Hooray!" Jake cheered. "She's back to normal." Unfortunately it came out rather louder than intended.

"Jake?" Miss Flockpockle called, peering down through the hole in the window boarding. "Is that you? Why aren't you in school?"

"We came to rescue you," Jake said. "You see..." he began to explain, but that was as far as he got. Blackbeard's grey stubbly face loomed into view behind Miss Flockpockle's head.

"Why, if it isn't that pesky little pigeon dropping and his interfering old dragon of a granny," he roared. "Don't you two ever give up?"

"Not while you're busy kidnapping teachers and using heads as basketballs," Granny snapped back. "Someone's got to keep you in line."

Blackbeard scratched his head. "How do you know about my special basketball?" He pointed a filthy finger at them. "You'd better not have touched it or I'll be slam dunking you straight into the slops bin. It'll be game over for you two, quicker than you can say 'Granny Shot'..."

The other pirates began to cheer.

"You tell 'em Blackbeard. Laser the lot of them! Squish 'em like fleas."

"Please, Miss Flockpockle," Jake begged. "You've got to get out of there. Before it turns nasty."

"I'm not scared of *them*," she said. "I'm a teacher. I'm used to bad behavior and silly fights."

"But they want to swap you for a rabbit," Jake said. "And then we'll have no one to teach our class. We'll be stuck with Cutthroat for the whole year."

"Mr. Cutthroat, did you say?" Miss Flockpockle broke off another section of window boarding and leaned out. "Has he got long curly hair and terrible breath?"

"Yes," Jake said. "That's him. You left him in charge of the class after Blackbeard zapped you with the Meltamax 4000."

"I remember now!" Miss Flockpockle cried. "It's all coming back to me. There was a funny pink cube thing..."

"It made you fall in love with him. It made you write crazy things like this." He pulled her letter out of his pocket and began to read:

"That's just one of the three thousand and eighty-four things I love about you.

Today has been the happiest day of my entire life — and the nicest smelling too. You should bottle your special pirate fragrance and sell it."

"Stop!" Miss Flockpockle cried. *Now* she looked

scared. "I don't want to hear any more. Get me out

of here!"

"The only place you're going is the Swap

Shop," Blackbeard roared. "And I'll be trading you

two troublemakers in for some rabbit food while I'm

there."

But Miss Flockpockle was already squeezing

through the gap in the window. She wriggled and

twisted her top half all the way through before

Blackbeard could stop her. He let out a furious

growl and lunged for her legs, but it was too late.

Jake and Granny stretched up their arms to catch

her, and the three of them landed in a tangled heap on the ground.

"Run!" Granny shouted as they picked themselves back up and sprinted off through a swarm of marshmallows. "Back to the landing field!"

"After them," came an angry pirate cry. "Don't let them get away!"

10

MELTAMAX 4000

"I'm sorry I didn't believe you, Jake," Miss

Flockpockle said, panting as they sprinted toward

the yellow spaceship. "You warned me about

Blackbeard, and I didn't listen."

"Right now I wish he *was* a figment of my

imagination," Jake said, looking back. The pirates

were red-faced and out of breath, staggering along

in their heavy black boots. But they weren't giving

up yet.

"Just wait 'til I get my hands on you," Blackbeard puffed. "I'll crush you like cosmic crackers. I'll pulp you like plasma peas." He shook his fist as he ran. "I'm gonna make comet custard out of your kidneys."

"If you're going to threaten us," Miss Flockpockle called back, "at least do it correctly. It's 'I'm going to' not 'I'm gonna.'"

"There's no time for grammar lessons," Jake shouted. "We're almost there!"

Mrs. Raymore's spaceship was in plain sight now. Out of the corner of his eye Jake saw Granny fetching the key from her pocket and pressing the unlock switch. They just might make it.

Jake raced up the steps and dived on board.

"Phew!" he cried. "Let's get out of here!"

Granny was right behind him. "Come on, Miss

Flockpockle," she called. "Hurry up! And watch out

for that rock!"

Miss Flockpockle glanced at the ground. "What

rock?" she asked. But nothing on Switchox was

where it should be.

"That one there!" Jake yelled.

Smack! Miss Flockpockle ran straight into a

floating pink boulder and flew backwards.

"Ha! That'll learn you." Blackbeard laughed,

coming up fast. "You'll never make it now."

Miss Flockpockle sat up with a groan.

"That'll *teach* you," she corrected him.

"Not *learn* you. If you're going to gloat at least do it properly."

Granny rolled her eyes. "Is she always like this?" she asked Jake, bounding back down the steps to help.

"No," he said, following behind. "She's usually worse."

Together they hauled the teacher onto her feet and dragged her on board, still muttering under her breath about the poor state of pirate education. Blackbeard thundered up the steps behind them.

"Quick, Granny, close the hatch!" Jake called. But it was too late. There was a big black boot blocking the way.

"Not so fast you pathetic pack of pigfish," the pirate said, forcing his way onto the ship.

Jake's heart sank. They'd never get away now.

"Fish don't swim in packs," Miss Flockpockle pointed out. "The correct term for a group of pigfish would be 'shoal' or 'school'. Although as there are only three of us I'm not sure..."

"Zip it," Blackbeard interrupted. "If I wanted a lesson on talking properly I'd..." He paused. "I don't know *what* I'd do actually. But it doesn't matter anyhow because I let my laser pistol do the talking for me." He patted his belt and let out a long sigh. "Or at least I would if I knew where it was. I must have left it in the bathroom again. I'm always doing that."

"You should go back for it," Jake suggested. "Before anyone else finds it."

Blackbeard scowled. "I don't think so. You're just waiting for me to leave so you can zoom off with Miss Fluffpuffle here."

"It's Flockpockle," the teacher said.

"Well, Miss Fatpaddle, let me tell you this. The only place you'll be zooming off to is the Swap Shop. Because I'm not leaving Switchox until I've got a new Fluffykins. Do you understand?"

"I understand that you're a rude, ignorant man who can't even get my name right," Miss Flockpockle said. She was wearing her 'cross face'.

Oh man, thought Jake. *Here we go again.*

"Do you know what?" Blackbeard said. "I think I liked you better when you were all lovey dovey. At least you did what you were told. Perhaps it's time for another burst of the Meltamax 4000." He turned to Long John Mercury who stood red-faced and spluttering in the doorway. "What do you think? One more blast?"

Long John Mercury shrugged. "Whatever you say, Captain. Maybe you should zap the lot of 'em.

Splat 'em like splimplets. It'll make life easier when it comes to trading 'em in."

Blackbeard grinned. "Excellent idea. You're not just a pretty ugly face, are you?" He waved the pink cube at Granny and Jake. "Which one shall I do first? That's the question."

"It would take more than a stolen machine to make *me* love you," Jake said, thinking hard. How were they going to get out of this one?

"Be quiet you fiddly little flea-freckle," Blackbeard snapped. "I've had enough of you. Prepare to be Meltamaxed."

Granny gasped. "You leave my grandson out of this. *I'm* the one you want. Put down the Meltamax and I'll come quietly."

"She's lying," Jake said. "Don't listen to her."

"What are you doing?" Granny hissed.

"I've got a plan," he whispered back. Long John Mercury had given him an idea but there wasn't time to explain.

"Hmm. I *could* leave your grandson out of it," Blackbeard said. "Or I could blast him with my new toy. No contest! I'm going to Meltamax him and get rid of the meddling maggot-mouth once and for all!"

11

THE NEW BOY

Jake stared at the Meltamax as he reached out a hand and felt along the floor with his fingers. If his plan didn't work he was in big trouble.

Blackbeard counted down, a huge grin stretched across his stubbly face. "Three... Two...One..."

Jake's fingers curled around the splimpet jar. He swung it up in front of his chest just as Blackbeard pressed the button. Then he held his breath, hoping the blast would backfire as planned.

Yes! There it was! A bright pink flash bounced off

the edge of the jar and crackled back toward the

pirate.

Blackbeard clutched at his heart. "What an

adorable creature," he said. "Why have they put

you in that jar? Poor thing. Let me get you out and

give you a cuddle."

Jake grinned at Granny, and she gave him the

thumbs up.

"Nice one!" she whispered.

Jake handed Blackbeard the jar, and he pulled

the splimpet out with a loud *pop!* The creature

attached itself firmly onto the pirate's chest.

"It's your new Fluffykins," Jake said.

"He's perfect." Blackbeard beamed. "My Fluffy-puffy-wuffykins. I'm gonna need a new tattoo now."

"You mean 'going to'," Miss Flockpockle reminded him. "Not 'gonna'."

"Something must have gone wrong, Captain," Long John Mercury piped up, scratching his chin and staring around the ship in confusion. "What about the rest of the zapping?"

Blackbeard shrugged. "That can wait. Just look at his wobbly blobbly face. Isn't he cute? I think he likes me." He put down the Meltamax so he could cuddle the splimpet. Granny pounced on the pink machine and pointed it at the pirates.

"You've got what you came for," she said. "So take your new Fluffykins and go, before I blast the rest of your crew."

Long John Mercury backed away. "Best do what she says, Captain. Let's get back to the spaceship and find a black felt pen to fix your tattoo. Even *I* can draw a horrible shapeless blob."

"Good idea," Blackbeard said. "Come on my precious bloblet. Let's take you home. We're going to be so happy together. I just know it."

Granny shut the hatch behind them and high-fived Jake.

"You were fantastic," she said.

"Good work, sir," Rillo said as the screen flickered back to life.

"Quick thinking," Miss Flockpockle agreed. "And as a special reward for saving me I'll only give you three math questions for our journey home. How does that sound?"

It didn't sound good at all. "You should rest first," Jake said. "Take a seat." He pointed to one of the pods and nodded at Rillo. "Have you got any more of that Saturn Sleeping Scent?" he whispered.

Rillo winked back. "Coming right up."

With Miss Flockpockle fast asleep Jake was able to enjoy non-stop cartoons and Moonfizz all the way back to the Moon. They made it safely through the Zip Tube without any more splimpet attacks and were soon back at Granny's.

"Almost there now," Jake told his teacher as they caught the lift down to the Zoomster platform. "We just need to pick up Granny's spaceship and return some lost property." But Miss Flockpockle was still dozy after her sleep and could only mutter, "I'm on the Moon...I'm actually standing on the Moon," over and over like a song stuck on 'repeat'.

The Mang was overjoyed to have his fourth head back and promised Granny a year's worth of free Zoomster travel as a reward. She, in turn, promised to pick up some more Earth bananas for him when she dropped Jake and Miss Flockpockle home.

They landed Granny's spaceship by the school bike sheds and hurried inside to rescue the class from Mr. Cutthroat. Everything seemed suspiciously quiet. Jake half expected to find his friends tied up in the cupboard or cowering in the corner. But he couldn't have been more wrong. The pirate was sitting at a spare desk, listening to one of the girls explaining division.

"So it's like sharing thirty-five treasure chests between five bloodthirsty pirates?" he said.

The girl nodded.

Cutthroat thought for a bit. "That makes seven

chests each."

The class cheered. Miss Flockpockle cleared her

throat and they all fell quiet again.

"Ah," sighed the pirate. "You're back. And I

was just startin' to get the hang of it. I never knew

learnin' could be such fun."

"Then why don't you stay and learn some

more?" someone suggested. "Can he, Miss

Flockpockle? Can he join our class?"

Miss Flockpockle stared at all the hopeful

faces.

"He'd have to have a bath and get some clean

clothes," she said.

The pirate stared down at his ripped trousers and sniffed. "I guess a bath wouldn't be *so* bad after all these years."

"And he'd have to learn some proper manners."

Cutthroat belched and scratched his armpit. "I suppose I'd have to give up my pirating ways too?"

Miss Flockpockle nodded.

He sighed. "To be honest, I'm getting a bit bored of all the fighting and cursing. Not to mention the smell. And the food is *terrible*. I'm always hungry."

"You can share my packed lunch," offered one of the boys.

"And mine," called another. "I've got cheese sandwiches."

Cutthroat grinned. "Well that settles it then. I'm gonna leave Blackbeard's gang and join Miss Flotpottle's learnin' crew instead."

"It's *Flockpockle*." Jake's teacher sighed. "And it's 'going to,' not 'gonna'."

"Sorry, Captain," Cutthroat said, wiping his nose on his sleeve.

Miss Flockpockle sighed again. "Oh dear. It's going to be a long term."

Jake giggled as Cutthroat dug out a fresh lump of earwax with Miss Flockpockle's marking pen. Lessons could never be as exciting as racing around the universe with Moon Granny. But with a real

pirate as a school classmate, they certainly

wouldn't be boring!

About The Author

Jaye Seymour is a Cambridge University English graduate and previous winner of the Commonwealth Short Story Competition. Her fiction has appeared in a number of publications on both sides of the Atlantic, including *The Guardian*, *Mslexia*, *The First Line*, *Short Fiction* and *Knowonder!* She was shortlisted for the 2013 Greenhouse Funny Prize and lives in Devon, England.

About Knowonder!

Knowonder is a leading publisher of engaging, daily content that drives literacy—the most important factor in a child's success.

Parents and educators use Knowonder tools and content to promote reading, creativity, and thinking skills in children from ages 0-12.

Knowonder's storybook collections and chapter books deliver original, compelling new stories every day, creating an opportunity for parents to connect to their children in ways that significantly improve their children's success.

Ultimately, Knowonder's mission is to eradicate illiteracy and improve education success through content that is affordable, accessible, and effective.

Learn more at www.knowonder.com

Printed in Great Britain
by Amazon